Craftily Ever After

#4

Dream Machine

By Martha Maker Illustrated by Xindi Yan

LITTLE SIMON
New York London Toronto Sydney New Delhi

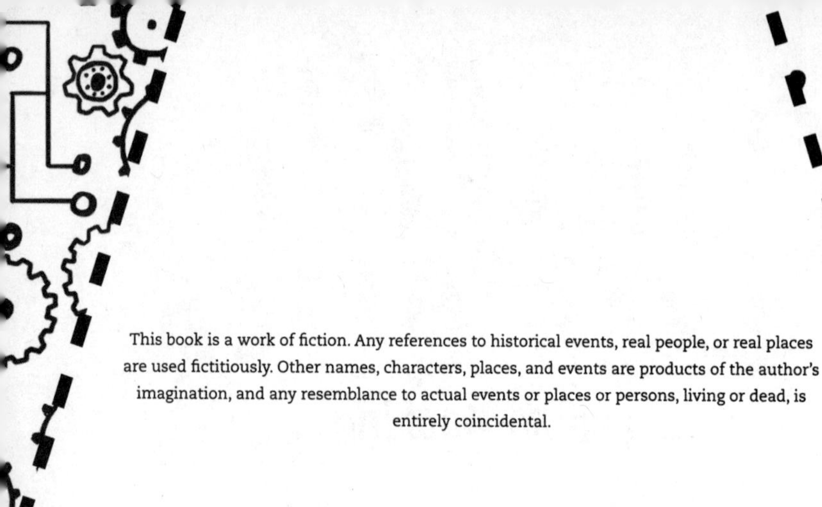

LITTLE SIMON
An imprint of Simon & Schuster Children's Publishing Division
1230 Avenue of the Americas, New York, New York 10020
First Little Simon hardcover edition August 2018

Designed by Laura Roode
The text of this book was set in Caecilia.
Manufactured in the United States of America 0718 FFG
2 4 6 8 10 9 7 5 3 1
Cataloging-in-Publication Data is available for this title from the Library of Congress.
ISBN 978-1-5344-1731-1 (hc)
ISBN 978-1-5344-1730-4 (pbk)
ISBN 978-1-5344-1732-8 (eBook)

CONTENTS

CHAPTER
1
1

What a Dream!

Rrrrrrrrrrrr . . .

Bella Diaz stepped on the gas. The engine roared and the race car zoomed forward.

Beaming happily, Bella adjusted a knob on the dashboard. She had designed and programmed the race car herself! Bella loved anything to do with computers: programming, coding, and beyond. And she'd always dreamed of being able to program her very own race car!

She gripped the steering wheel with her purple leather racing gloves as she sped down the race track and into a tight turn.

Just then a light flashed red. *Warning! Warning!*

Oh no! She had taken the turn a little too fast. Bella spun the wheel, leaned hard, and . . .

THUMP!

Bella opened her eyes. She was on the floor next to her bed, twisted up in her blankets.

For a moment she was completely confused. Then she realized what had happened.

Whew, what a dream! Her heart was still racing, thinking about flying around the track. And thinking about that amazing car.

She untangled herself and stood up. Glancing at her alarm clock, she saw that it was still early.

Well, I might as well get up, thought Bella. *I could grab a few more minutes of sleep, but there's no way I'd have a dream that awesome again!*

CHAPTER
2

Robots or Race Cars?

That morning Bella was the first to arrive in Ms. Gibbons's classroom. Still thinking about her dream, she pulled out a notebook. She began sketching a picture of her race car. She wanted to capture all the details before the dream faded.

"Cool car!"

Bella looked up. Her friend Emily

Adams was leaning over the edge of her desk, trying to get a better look at Bella's drawing.

"Thanks," Bella replied. "Last night I dreamed I was driving it. But it was also sort of driving itself because I wrote the code so it would follow the race course. Only I might have miscalculated the turning axis, because—"

"Whoa, whoa, whoa." Emily held up a hand. "Slow down, Bella. You're light-years ahead of me when it comes to programming. Though, if you want some help with the engineering, I'm game. There are some pretty simple things you can do to make the car go faster. Like tapering the back, or adding a spoiler."

Bella grinned. "When I do build my dream car, I'll definitely want you on the design team."

"What design team?" asked their friend Sam Sharma, who had just arrived. Sam loved to paint and draw. Clearly, the word "design" had gotten his attention.

Before Bella could explain, the bell rang. There was a sparkly purple blur in the classroom doorway as Maddie Wilson dashed in. She was wearing a sequined dress that Bella was pretty sure had been pink the day before.

Bella smiled. Leave it to Maddie to reinvent her outfit overnight!

Maddie slid into her seat, turned

to her three best friends, and whispered, "What did I miss?"

"We'll tell you at lunch," answered Bella, Emily, and Sam at once.

Over sandwiches, Bella showed Sam and Maddie her race car sketch.

"It's from my dream last night," she explained. "I was thinking maybe it could be the inspiration for our next project!"

The four friends met regularly to do craft projects together, and they were always on the lookout for new ideas.

DISTRICT-WIDE
ROBOT-BUILDING
CONTEST!
DAN
5

Just then two older girls walked by. They were carrying stacks of neon green flyers. But it wasn't just the color that caught Bella's eye; it was the picture of a robot! If there was anything Bella loved more than the idea of programming a race car, it was robots!

Bella watched the girls go from table to table, passing them out. She couldn't wait until the girls got to their table.

But by the time the bell rang, no flyer. And the girls had already left the cafeteria.

Bella was disappointed. What was the robot flyer for? And why did the older girls skip their table? None of her friends seemed to notice—they were still discussing different types of cars they could build.

On the way back to their classroom, a flash of neon green caught Bella's eye. A flyer! It was taped to the wall above a drinking fountain. Bella read it quickly.

DISTRICT-WIDE ROBOT-BUILDING CONTEST!

Mason Creek Elementary School will be entering a team!

All interested students should come to a meeting at lunch tomorrow!

Interested? You bet I am, thought Bella.

CHAPTER
3
DISTRICT-WIDE
ROBOT-BUILDIN
CONTEST!

The Robotics Team

When the bell rang for lunch the next day, Bella told her friends to go ahead without her. She thought about inviting them to come to the meeting with her. But she decided to check it out herself. If it turned out to be as awesome as she hoped, she could always recruit them later.

Bella found the meeting room.

In her enthusiasm, she threw the door open with a *BANG!*

All eyes turned toward her. There were about ten kids there already, including the two girls who were handing out the flyers. One of them gave Bella a funny look.

"Are you lost?" the girl asked in a tone that made Bella feel like she was about five years old.

"I . . . I don't think so," said Bella, now nervous. "Is this the robotics club?"

A tall, skinny boy laughed. "It's not a *club*. It's a team," he corrected her.

CALENDAR

"That's . . . uh . . . that's what I meant," stammered Bella.

"You can't join. You're too young," said the girl who had asked if Bella was lost.

"Yeah, no little kids allowed," added the tall boy.

"Oh . . . okay," said Bella, completely embarrassed. She turned around to leave. But then she stopped herself. She *really* wanted to know more about this robot-building contest.

Bella turned back around and took a deep breath. "But . . . the poster said *all interested students*," she managed to say.

"Bryce? Naomi? She has a point," said someone from the back of the room. Bella looked and saw that there was a teacher there.

"The rules state that the contest is *recommended* for students ages ten to twelve, but that's only a guideline. So, it's not against the rules for younger students to participate."

"But, Mrs. Jacobs . . . ," complained Naomi.

The teacher held up a hand. "Let's not waste time arguing. We have a lot to get done. Naomi and Bryce, as team captains, will you please explain the rules of the contest?"

Bella felt her heart racing as the two older students rattled off the rules of the robot-building contest. She saw some of the other kids taking notes, so she pulled out her notebook and did the same.

When they got to the end of the rules, Mrs. Jacobs asked, "Any questions?"

Several hands shot up.

"Are they going to provide us with a field set-up kit?"

"Can we use a smartphone as the controller?"

"Is there a limit to how many team members can be in the pit?"

Bella's eyes widened. It seemed like everyone had been on a robotics team before. Everyone except her.

Finally the meeting ended. As Bella put her notebook away, she couldn't help noticing a couple of the kids whispering. Were they talking about her?

Bella sighed. She trudged back to her classroom, feeling defeated. Maybe she should have just walked away the first time.

CHAPTER
4

Second Chances

When school let out, Bella went home, changed her clothes, and then went to wait for her friends at the craft clubhouse in her back-yard. As soon as Sam, Maddie, and Emily arrived, the four of them fell into their familiar habit of joking, laughing, and sharing new craft project ideas.

Bella smiled. It felt *so* much better to be at *this* meeting.

"Where were you at lunch, Bella?" asked Maddie. "We came up with the best idea and you totally missed it."

Bella hesitated. Did she even

want to tell her friends about her embarrassing experience with the robotics team? She settled on a shortened version of the story and just told her friends that she'd seen the flyer about a robotics team so she'd gone to check it out.

"There's a robotics team?" asked Emily. "Are you going to join?"

"Probably not," said Bella breezily. "Anyway, what's our idea?"

"Well, we still want to make a car," said Sam. "But we came up with the idea of using lighter materials and making a bunch of small model cars. That way, we

could power them with balloons and race them."

"What do you think?" Maddie asked Bella.

Bella hesitated. Balloon-powered cars couldn't do nearly as many cool things as computer-powered cars. But racing sounded fun, and they had to start somewhere!

"Sounds great," she told her friends. "Let's go look for materials!"

After a trip to Bella's kitchen recycling bin and a spin through the craft supply containers in the clubhouse, the friends had assembled lots of good items for their project: plastic bottles and wood scraps for

the car frames, plus bottle tops, jar lids, and big buttons from Maddie's stash of sewing supplies for wheels. They also collected all sorts of decorations, paints, and fasteners.

While Bella was organizing everything into neat piles, Sam came over to her.

“Are you really not going to join the robotics team?” he asked. “That sounds like your dream team!”

Bella shrugged. “All the kids were older than me. And they’ve probably

all built tons of robots before," she said.

"Bet they haven't starred in a rock band or tie-dyed a shirt for the mayor," Sam said with a wink.

Bella laughed. Maybe Sam was right. Maybe she was psyching *her-self* out. Maybe . . . she'd give the robotics team another shot.

CHAPTER
5

Hold That Thought

And Bella did give it another shot. The following week, she was back in Mrs. Jacobs's classroom.

"Glad you came back," said Mrs. Jacobs with a smile.

Bella smiled, but she wondered if Mrs. Jacobs would be the *only* one who was happy to see her.

This time Bella had made a point

of getting there early and finding a good seat. As the older kids arrived, though, she couldn't help but notice that none of them said hello or sat down near her.

"Okay, let's get started," said Mrs. Jacobs. "So, the contest challenge has been announced and it is a 'green' one. This means our robot will need to do two things to help the environment. Why don't we start by brainstorming ideas?"

Bella may have been obsessed with all things computer and electronics, but she also definitely cared about the environment. She raised her hand.

Mrs. Jacobs asked the robotics team captains to run the brainstorming session. Naomi called on people to share their ideas, and Bryce wrote the ideas down on the board.

"Let's see," said Naomi, looking around the room. "Kimaya?"

“Our robot could monitor sunlight and move plants in response, so they get the optimum amount of sunlight.”

“Great idea,” said Naomi. Bella waved her hand, but Naomi called on a boy named Angelo instead.

“Maybe our robot could run on solar power?” he suggested.

“Very cool,” said Naomi.

Finally, Naomi pointed at Bella.

"Me?" asked Bella, feeling a little self-conscious. "My name is Bella. You guys have a lot of great ideas. I have one to add, which is that our robot could—"

RIIIIIIINNNNGGGG!

At the sound of the bell, everyone

jumped up and grabbed their things. Everyone except Bella, who just sat there in disbelief.

Mrs. Jacobs came over and put a hand on her shoulder. "I'll bet you had a good idea. Can you hang on to it for next time?"

Bella nodded, but she wasn't sure. The older kids probably wouldn't even like her idea. Plus, they had so many good ideas of their own, they didn't need a little *kid*'s help.

Almost as if she had read Bella's mind, Mrs. Jacobs added, "'Though she be but little, she is fierce.'"

Bella looked up, confused.

"It's from Shakespeare," explained Mrs. Jacobs. "It's my way of saying that you matter. So, don't doubt yourself, okay?" She winked at Bella.

"Okay," said Bella. But she didn't wink back.

CHAPTER
6

Bella Breaks Down

After school, Bella and her mom went to the supermarket. Bella's mom did the grocery shopping, but she left the cooking up to Bella's dad, who was a chef.

In the produce aisle, Mrs. Diaz suggested, "Why don't you get the fruits and I'll get the veggies."

"Okay," said Bella. She selected

a pineapple, a bunch of bananas, and a bag of apples. Then she saw that mangoes were on sale. But as Bella took a mango from the display pile . . .

THUMP! SPLAT!

Several mangoes rolled off and landed on the floor. One was overripe and burst when it hit the ground, splattering Bella and other shoppers with sticky juice.

"I'm so sorry!" Bella bent down to pick up the mangoes. As she did, she dropped everything else she was trying to balance: the pine-apple, the bananas, and the bag of apples. The fruit went flying in different directions.

"Are you okay, sweetie?" asked a store employee, coming over to help.

Bella nodded. The employee was just trying to be nice, but he made Bella feel like a helpless little kid.

Just then Bella's mom appeared, holding a bunch of kale.

"Bella, *que pasó*? What happened?" she asked.

"I . . . I was just getting some mangoes, but then everything fell. . . ." Bella felt so frustrated. She couldn't do anything right, and now here she was about to bawl like a baby in the middle of the produce aisle!

Her mom helped her collect everything. "There we go!" she announced once all the fruit was in the shopping cart.

"What's wrong, Bella?" asked her mom after they moved on to the bread aisle. "You're so quiet today."

Bella shrugged, but said nothing.

They passed a shopping cart with a little boy in the seat. Bella's mother smiled at him, then turned to Bella. "I don't remember you ever sitting still in the cart. You just wanted to *push* the cart. You used to pretend it was a race car, remember?"

Bella smiled at the memory. But then it made her think of building the race cars, which made her think of Sam's suggestion about the robotics team, which made her think about that team meeting again. And that memory *didn't* make her smile.

"It's just hard sometimes," she told her mom. "I'm too big for little kid stuff, but I'm too little for anyone to take me seriously." And the next thing Bella knew, it all came tumbling out: the flyers, the robotics team meeting, everything.

"I should probably just quit," she told her mom. "I mean, it's not like they're going to let me do anything—they didn't even want to hear my ideas! And they don't need a *little kid* messing things up. I mean, you saw what happened with the fruit. I'd probably drop their robot or break it—"

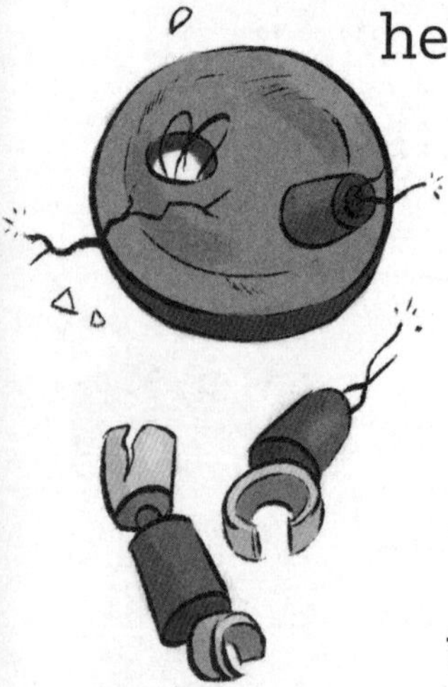

Bella's mom cut her off. "Do you know how your father got his big break?" she asked.

"No," said Bella. "How?"

"Well, he was in culinary school, and every student was required to prepare the same dish for a famous chef. Your father read the

instructions again and again, but something didn't look right to him. The recipe called for a *tablespoon* of salt, and your dad was pretty sure this would be overpowering. Finally, he trusted his intuition and made the adjustment—to a *teaspoon* of salt—and turned in his dish."

"What happened?" asked Bella.

"The famous chef went down the line of dishes like this." Bella's mom pretended to take a spoonful of soup, then made a pained face.

"Again and again, until he came to your father's dish."

Bella's mom took another pretend sip. This time, she beamed happily. "That famous chef offered your father his very first job. And you know what he told your dad? 'Anyone can chop up ingredients. But a true artist uses his mind, not just his hands.'"

"That's true when it comes to programming, too," said Bella. She thought for a moment. She'd give the robotics team *one* more shot.

CHAPTER
7

The Dream Machine

That Saturday the craft clubhouse came to life—loudly—as all four friends sawed, sanded, painted, and decorated their race cars.

Emily, the master builder, was in charge of wheel alignment. She carefully inspected each car to ensure a smooth ride. When she finished, the friends lined up their cars to admire them.

Sam's was, of course, beautifully painted with bright swirls of color. He had named his Rainbow Racer.

Maddie's car was purple and paisley and had a sequined fabric racing skirt around the bottom. Hers was called the Fast and the Fabulous.

Emily's car was called Solid Gold since it was *definitely* solid and Emily had spray-painted nuts and bolts gold and applied them to her car.

Bella called her car the Dream Machine.

"What are all those doodads you've got on there?" asked Maddie.

"My Dream Machine doesn't have 'doodads,'" said Bella. "Those are sensors that can measure the amount of air left in its tank, plus compressed air and also a hose to reinflate it!"

Everyone was super impressed.

"I think it's race time!" Emily said excitedly.

The four friends carried their cars out to Bella's driveway. Using chalk, they marked a starting line, race track, and finish line. Maddie brought along a checkered starting flag she had made too.

With balloons inflated, they positioned the four cars next to one another. Together they chanted, “On your marks, get set . . . GO!”

Everyone let go of their balloons and jumped back.

Three cars blasted off.

But the Dream Machine sputtered. Then scooted. Then stopped only an inch from the starting line.

Bella picked it up while her friends chased after their speeding cars. She felt a rush of the same embarrassment.

If she couldn't make a simple balloon-powered car, how would she be able to make it on the robotics team?

CHAPTER 8

Less Is More

"I don't understand," said Bella, studying her car. The sensors were still in position. The refill tank was full, so maybe the sensor malfunctioned?

"Try it again," said Emily, who had returned with the others to the starting line. Bella inflated the balloon again, set the car in position, and . . . nothing.

"Ugh!" Bella kicked the Dream Machine in frustration. One of the sensors fell off, making things worse.

Maddie picked up Bella's car and the broken sensor and handed both to her friend. "Try it now?" she suggested.

"I just did!" said Bella.

"No. I mean try it now that a piece is missing," explained Maddie. "I didn't want to say anything before because your car *looked* so cool. But you know what they say: Sometimes less is more."

Bella raised an eyebrow. Maddie's usual rule, especially when it came to accessorizing, was: *more* is more. But Bella decided to give her car another try.

This time the car actually moved! Not very fast, but it was clear Maddie had a point. Without the additional weight, the car could actually roll.

"To the clubhouse!" yelled Bella.

"Don't you want to race again?" asked Sam.

Bella shook her head. "You guys go ahead. I've got to hop online and do some research first!"

Half an hour later, Bella rejoined her friends in the driveway.

"Whoa!" said Maddie when she saw Bella's car. The car had none of the "doodads" from before. No bells, no whistles, no compressed-air tank—nothing.

"I know what you're thinking," said Bella. "How can it be *my* car when it looks so low tech? But here's what I learned from my research. Race car designers don't just make cars sleek to look cool. They do it to minimize drag and wind resistance. They also select specific

wheel sizes for performance, and try to eliminate extraneous ergonomic impediments."

"Um, English, please?" said Sam.

Bella flipped her car over and showed them the underside. "See? I removed the extra tank to make it much lighter than before. And I

made the wheels bigger, so my car would roll faster and be less likely to skid."

"Well, let's test out your theory!" said Maddie excitedly.

Again the friends inflated their balloons and lined up their cars.

"On your marks, get set, GO!"

This time, all four cars shot forward, with one car taking a distinct lead over the others: the new-and-improved Dream Machine. Cheering, the four friends ran after them, all the way to the finish line.

Maybe I do have something to contribute to that robotics team after all, Bella thought happily.

CHAPTER
9

The Big Day Disaster

Week after week, Bella kept showing up for robotics meetings. The team's robot was looking really cool. Most of the time, Bella just did whatever the older kids instructed her to do. Occasionally she'd ask a question—she really did want to learn more about robotics, after all!

When the day of the competition

finally came, Bella's mom drove her to the town hall.

Bella took a deep breath and walked in. Throughout the halls there were lots of adults and older kids in team T-shirts yelling, cheering, and carrying half-assembled robots.

When Bella finally found the exhibit hall, she gasped at the sight of it. There were booths everywhere, each with a team of kids, a presentation explaining their project, and

a robot on a display table. There were robots rolling, robots climbing, robots printing out data results, and so many other cool projects.

"Bella! Over here!"

Bella turned. There was Mrs. Jacobs, wearing a bright green MASON CREEK ROBOTICS TEAM T-shirt. The next thing she knew, Bella was wearing one too. It was big on her, but Bella was thrilled. Now she felt like she was officially part of the team!

There was just one problem: The *team* wasn't working very well as a team. Bryce was upset and Naomi was frantic. All the other kids were crowded around a smartphone, offering suggestions to a girl named Jenna. She was trying to get the robot to work, but she wasn't succeeding.

"Jenna! Shut it down and start over."

"Jenna, press one-two-three at once. That will override the system."

"Just turn it off. Not the phone, the bot. You need to reboot it."

Meanwhile, the robot seemed to be trying to respond to several commands at once. They had programmed it to move until it detected light on its solar panels. Then it was supposed to go retrieve a potted plant, bring it to the light source, and position it accordingly. Instead, it was rolling back and forth under the light source the team had set up. It kept knocking over potted plants. Dirt was spilling everywhere!

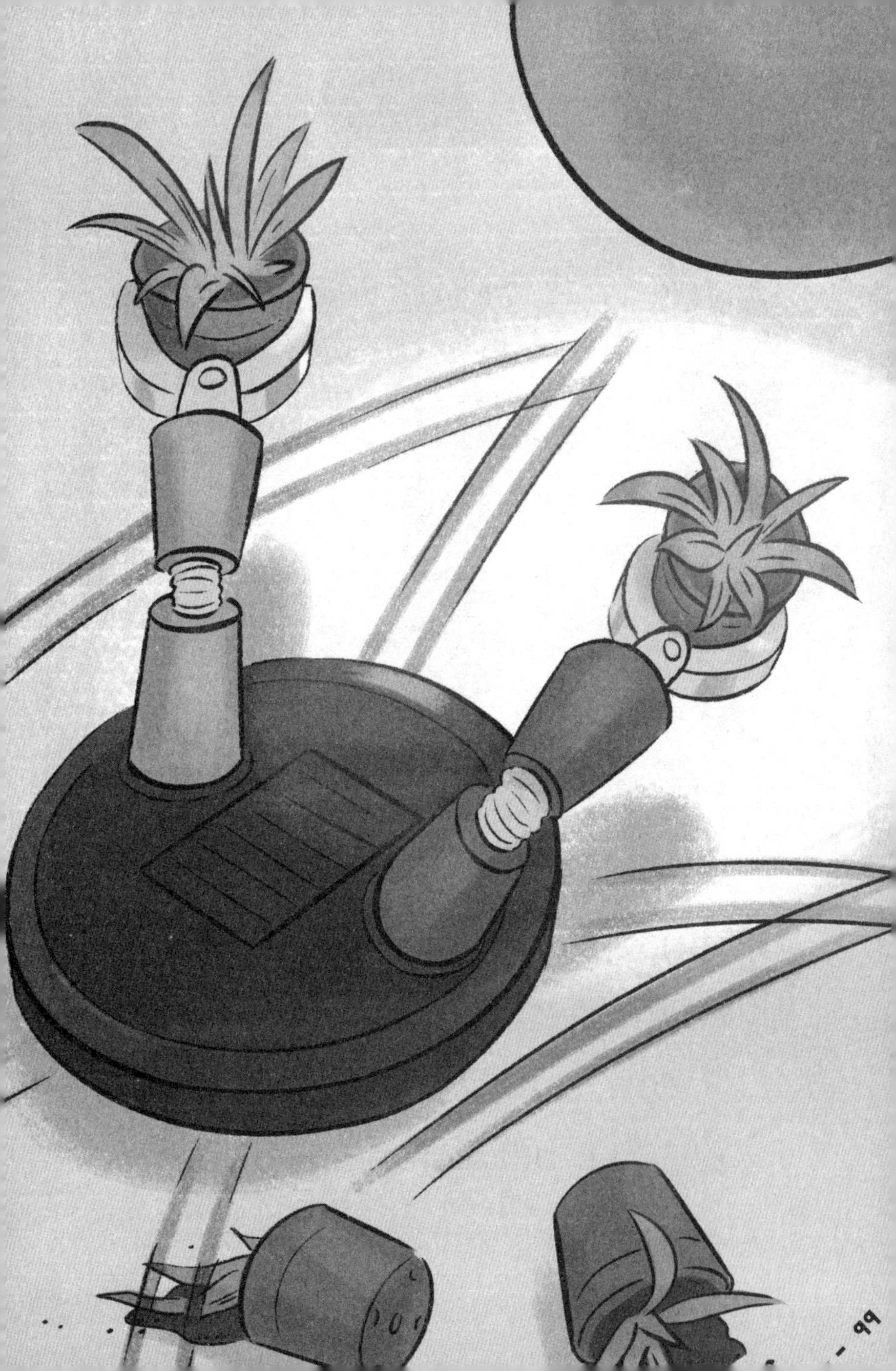

“This is a disaster,” wailed Bryce.

“We have to get it together!” said Naomi. “We are up for judging in five minutes.”

“I don’t know what to do,” said Jenna. “It’s not listening to me!”

Just then Bella had a thought.

"Um . . . could I try something?" she asked Jenna.

Jenna looked up from the screen, startled. But she seemed to realize that she wasn't going to be able to get the robot to work. She handed the phone to Bella.

"Thanks," said Bella. She pulled up the string of commands on the phone and quickly began to edit it. When she was finished, she handed the phone back to Jenna. She swept the dirt off the display table and put the plant into the robot's arms.

"Try it now," she told Jenna.

Jenna did as she was told . . . and so did the robot.

"Woo-hoo!" All the team members began to cheer as the robot

started moving toward the light source, then rotated the plant into position.

Just then the judges arrived at their booth. Bella thought they looked impressed as they took notes.

As soon as the judges had moved on, all eyes turned to Bella.

"How did you get it to work?" asked Naomi.

Bella smiled and showed her teammates the string of commands.

"I realized that we had added several unnecessary steps to the equation. It occurred to me that we might be more successful if we cut them out and streamlined it. Sometimes less is more," she added.

"Nice work," said Naomi with a genuine smile.

Now hopefully *less* would be *more* to the judges, who were already totaling everyone's scores.

CHAPTER 10

Dreams Come True

"Are we too late?" asked Sam, running up to Bella. Maddie, Emily, and Bella's parents followed seconds later.

"Nope," said Bella. "Check it out."

She borrowed the phone controller from Jenna and put the robot into action. Once again, it performed perfectly.

"That is so cool!" said Emily.

Bella smiled. Now *this* was a dream machine.

A crowd was gathering around the judging stand. The judges had posted the results!

Naomi ran over, and Bella and

the rest of the team waited with bated breath.

When Naomi ran back, Bella burst out, “So? How did we do?!”

Naomi smiled. “Our team won the silver cup—we got second place overall!”

The Mason Creek Robotics Team jumped up and down and cheered.

Then Naomi turned to Bella. "Bella, I'm sorry for the way I treated you when you first joined the team."

"So am I," added Bryce. "We should have given you more of a chance from the start. After all, if it hadn't been for you, we would have finished in last place—not second!"

"Thanks, guys. Although I wish we had come in first," Bella admitted.

Naomi laughed. "Well, we came

ason Creek
botics Team
Mason Cr
Robotics T

in fifth last year, so this is a big win for us! And next year maybe we *will* come in first. You're staying on the team, right?"

Bella raised her eyebrows. "Well, yeah, I guess," she said, both surprised and flattered. "I actually have an idea that might be fun to try out. Have you guys ever programmed a race car?"

Naomi and Bryce's eyes got wide. "A race car robot?! That sounds awesome!" said Naomi.

Bella smiled. She was really happy she hadn't given up on the robotics team—or on her Dream Machine. As it turned out, sometimes you just had to work a little harder for your dreams!

How to Make . . .
A Balloon-Powered Race Car

What you need:

Balloon
Flexible straws (3)
Tape
Water bottle
Bottle caps (4)
Sponge
Scissors
Barbecue skewers or chopsticks (2)

Step 1:

Make the jet by putting the long end of a flexible straw into the balloon.

Step 2:

Use tape to secure the straw and the balloon and to make sure no air will escape.

Step 3:

Lay the water bottle down. With scissors, poke two holes in the bottle. The holes should be directly across from each other on the part of the bottle that will be the back of the car.

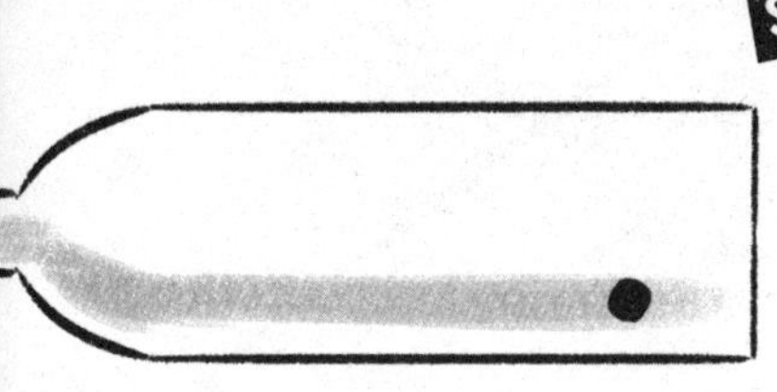

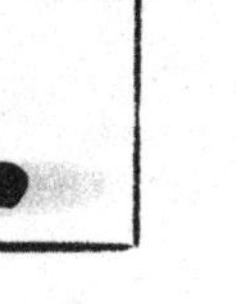

Step 4:

Slide a straw through the two holes. This is the axle. Adjust the axle so it goes straight across.

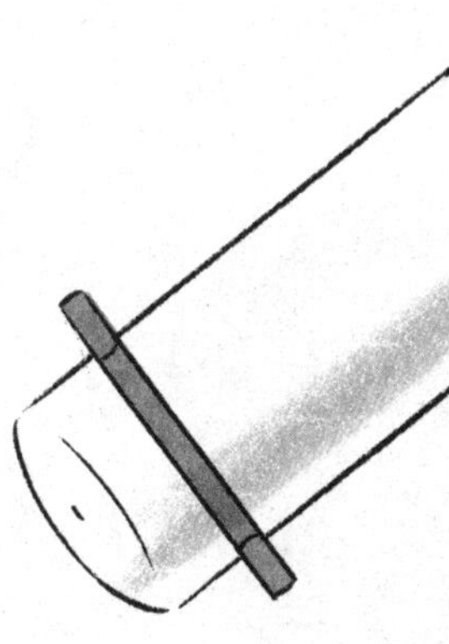

Repeat steps 3 and 4 at the top of the bottle, which will be the front of the car.

Step 6:

Slide a barbecue skewer through each straw.

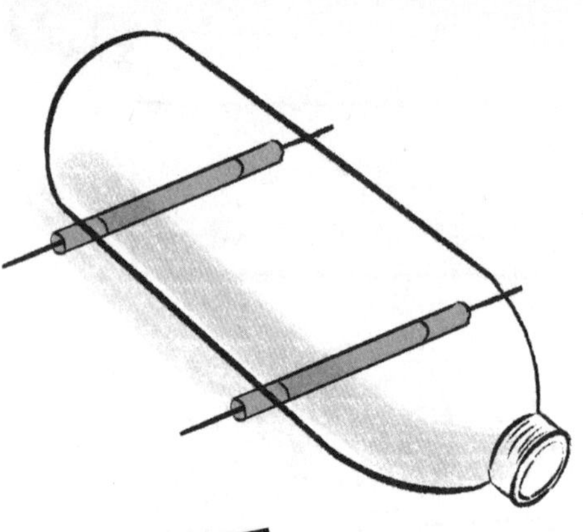

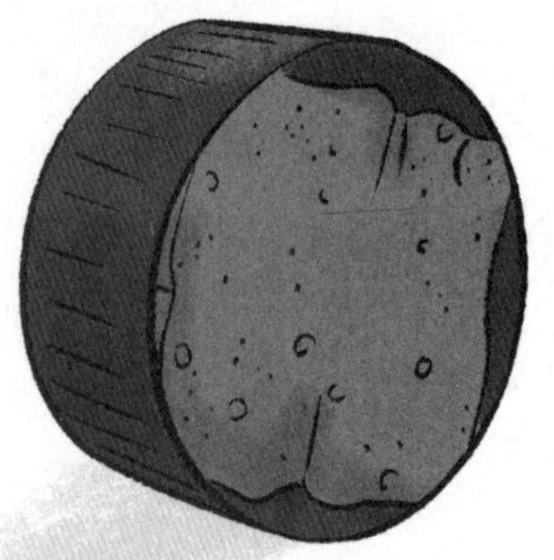

Step 7:

Cut your sponge into squares that will fit into the bottle caps. Then wedge a square of sponge into each bottle cap to make the wheels.

Step 8:

Use a spare skewer to poke holes into the center of each sponge.

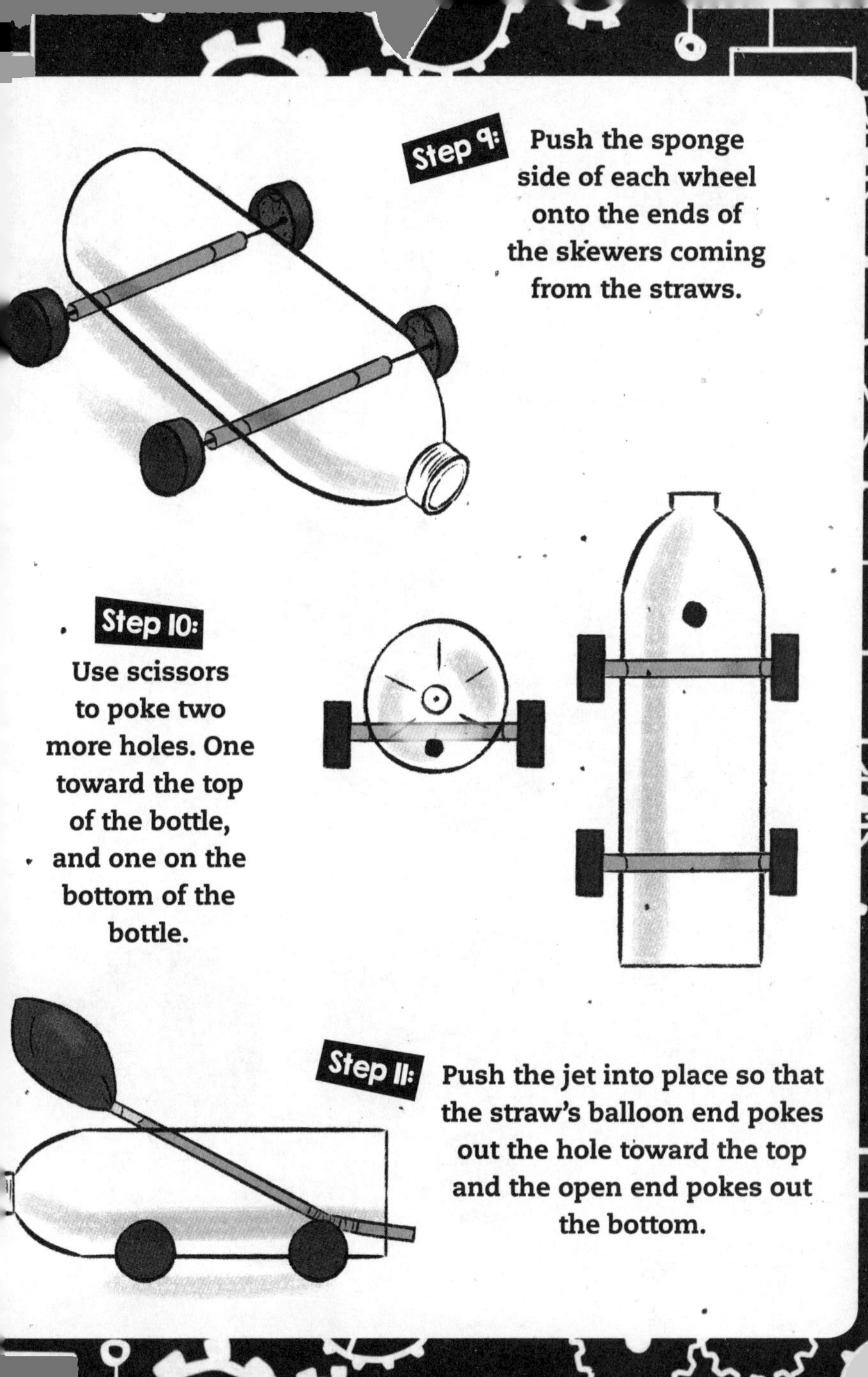

Step 9: Push the sponge side of each wheel onto the ends of the skewers coming from the straws.

Step 10: Use scissors to poke two more holes. One toward the top of the bottle, and one on the bottom of the bottle.

Step 11: Push the jet into place so that the straw's balloon end pokes out the hole toward the top and the open end pokes out the bottom.

Step 12:

Blow up the balloon by blowing through the straw, then quickly put your finger over the end of the straw to stop air from escaping.

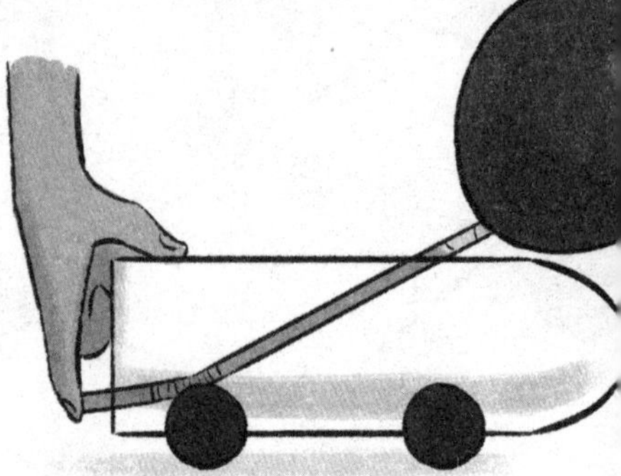

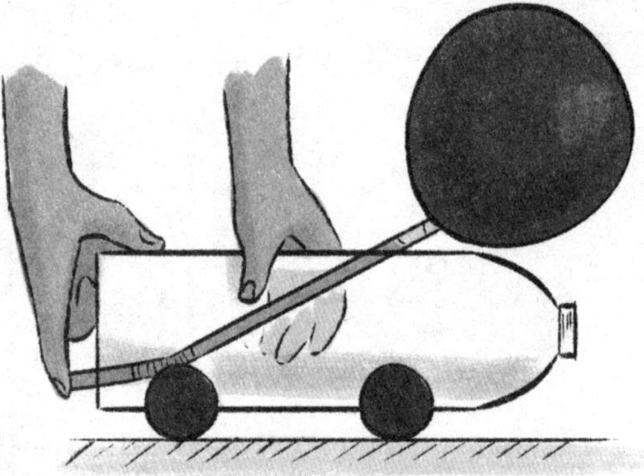

Step 13:

Put the car on a smooth surface.

Step 14:

Let go!

Here's a sneak peek at the next Craftily Ever After book!

The next day, Emily woke up still thinking about dogs. She really wanted one. But how could she convince her parents? She remembered what Sam said about it being a big responsibility. What if . . . ? That was it! She had an idea!

Later that morning, Emily called Sam and excitedly explained her plan.

"If I pitch in more at home, my parents will see how responsible I am," she said. "Then they couldn't possibly say no to a dog. I'll take out the garbage and unload the dish-washer without being asked, set the table, and—"

"Okay, but how will you show them you know how to care for a dog?" asked Sam.

"Well, I could . . ." Emily hadn't thought about that.

"You could practice by helping me with Bibi," suggested Sam.